NICKELODEON

DORA the EXPLORER®

W9-BFF-701

So Many Butterflies!

by Lara Bergen
illustrated by Warner McGee

Ready-to-Read

Simon Spotlight/Nickelodeon

New York   London   Toronto   Sydney

Based on the TV series *Dora the Explorer* ® as seen on Nick Jr. ®

SIMON SPOTLIGHT
An imprint of Simon & Schuster Children's Publishing Division
1230 Avenue of the Americas, New York, New York 10020
© 2010 Viacom International Inc. All rights reserved. NICK JR., *Dora the Explorer*, and all
related titles, logos and characters are registered trademarks of Viacom International Inc.
For information about special discounts for bulk purchases,
please contact Simon & Schuster Special Sales at
1-866-506-1949 or business@simonandschuster.com.
Manufactured in the United States of America
0710 LAK
8 10 9 7
Library of Congress Cataloging-in-Publication Data
Bergen, Lara.
So many butterflies! / by Lara Bergen ; illustrated by Warner McGee. —1st ed.
p. cm. — (Ready-to-read ; #22)
"Dora the Explorer."
ISBN 978-1-4169-9080-2
I. McGee, Warner. II. Dora the Explorer (Television program) III. Title.
PZ7.B44985So 2010
[E]—dc22
2009004225

Hi! I am  !
DORA

I have a  .
CAMERA

And so does my friend  .
BOOTS

We are taking
PICTURES

for our seasons  !
BOOK

Look at all the pretty ⬤ 🌷 !
PURPLE FLOWERS

Do you know which season it is?

Yes! It is spring!

🐵 and I love spring!
BOOTS

Do you?

Mmm!  smell so good!

FLOWERS

Let's take PICTURES of the FLOWERS

for our seasons BOOK !

Look!  wants to take
BOOTS

a  of something else
PICTURE

that is  .
PURPLE

A  !
BUTTERFLY

and I love .

BOOTS   BUTTERFLIES

Do you?

I wonder what other colors

of we can find?

BUTTERFLIES

I see a  !
BLUE BUTTERFLY

Do you?

And I see 3  in a nest, too!

THREE BLUE EGGS

 found a
BOOTS   GREEN BUTTERFLY

by the .

POND

Good job, !

BOOTS

What else at the  POND is GREEN ?
Don't forget to take a PICTURE,

BOOTS.

What color is this 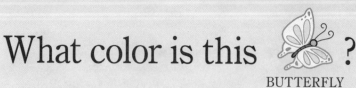 ?

! And so are the .

Let's take a  PICTURE

of the DUCKLINGS , too!

Look! I see an   .
ORANGE BUTTERFLY

And  found a  .
BOOTS   BUTTERFLY

It is  just like his  !
RED   BOOTS

Uh-oh!

Do you see ? SWIPER

SWIPER wants to swipe

my CAMERA !

We have to stop  SWIPER !

Say " SWIPER , no swiping!"

Yay! We stopped !
SWIPER

But look at that big 🌧️ ☁️.
RAIN   CLOUD

🦋🦋 do not like the 🌧️.
BUTTERFLIES   RAIN

Do you see a dry place

the 🦋🦋 can go?
BUTTERFLIES

That  ? Good idea!
CAVE
Hurry! Let's go!

Yay! The 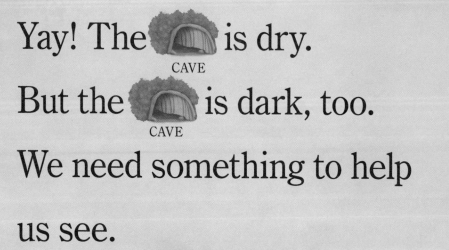 is dry.
But the is dark, too.
We need something to help

us see.

What does 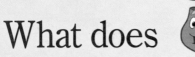 have
BACKPACK

that can help us see in the

dark  ?
CAVE

A  ! Yes!
FLASHLIGHT

The  has stopped.
RAIN

The ⚪ is coming out.
SUN

And look! There is a 🌈!
RAINBOW

 and I love .

BOOTS   RAINBOWS

And so do the  !

BUTTERFLIES

What a great  PICTURE

for our seasons BOOK !